BILLY AND ANT FALL OUT

BILLY GROWING UP SERIES: FRIENDSHIP and PRIDE

James Minter

Helen Rushworth – Illustrator

www.billygrowingup.com

MINTER PUBLISHING LIMITED

Minter Publishing Limited (MPL)
4 Lauradale, Bracknell RG12 7DT

Hardback ISBN: 978-1-910727-119

eBook ISBN: 978-1-910727-102

Paperback ISBN: 978-1-910727-089

Illustrations copyright © Helen Rushworth

Printed and bound in Great Britain by Ingram Spark,
Milton Keynes

<<<<<<

*DEDICATED to those whose arrogant pride
stops them from doing the right thing.*

This book belongs to

....

I give it

stars

1

BILLY AND ANT FALL OUT

"Have you seen this?" Billy pointed at the skateboard magazine while his dog Jacko licked his paw. "It's awesome. It's got go-faster wheels with extra-special bearings. It'll go really fast."

Billy rubbed Jacko's head, "Shall I get you one? I've seen loads of dogs on YouTube riding skateboards. I'm sure you can do it; you're a clever boy." He hugged Jacko around the neck. "Yes, you are." Billy buried his face in the dog's soft golden fur.

Then Billy stood. "Come on, boy. Up." He patted himself on the chest. "Come on, right up."

Jacko stood on his hind legs and rested his front paws on Billy's shoulders.

"See, I said you were clever."

The back door latch clicked, and both Billy and Jacko turned to see who'd come. Ant, Billy's best friend, walked in.

"What are you two doing?" Ant said. "Practicing ballroom dancing? D'you know why dogs don't make good dancers? Because they've got two left feet!" Ant laughed.

Billy made a cheesy-grin face; Jacko stayed where he was.

"Anyway, who's the girl out of you two?" Ant said.

"You're the only girl around here," Billy said, swinging a playful punch at Ant's arm.

Jacko dropped to the ground and woofed. Ant hit Billy back, and Jacko woofed again.

"Shush, Jacks; we're only messing." Billy knelt beside him. "Me and Ant are best mates." He looked toward Ant, who stood staring at the magazine. "Aren't we?"

"What? Sorry mate. Have you seen this skateboard? It's well nice. I'd love one like that." Ant picked up the magazine and hugged it, off in a dream world where he skateboarded like a professional.

"Yeah, but look at the price." Billy brought his friend back to reality. "It'll take two birthdays and a Christmas to save for it."

Longingly, they both looked at the picture. Billy dreamed of the day he might own one.

"We'll get one. You'll see." Ant sounded sure, but they had no idea if or when it might happen.

Billy turned to Ant. "I know, let's promise that whoever gets a board first lets the other have a go."

They held out their crooked little fingers and hooked them together. "I promise," they said in unison.

Billy looked down at Jacko as the dog pushed his way in between them. "But I don't think you'll be riding a board for a while, and at that price, neither will I."

Jacko only panted as Billy closed the magazine.

Billy looked to Ant for inspiration, "So, what are we doing today?"

"Fancy a bike ride?" Ant said.

"Yeah, maybe, but not down the park." Billy cringed at the thought of running into the bully who had stolen his twenty-pound note a few weeks ago.

"Why not? Eddy won't be there."

"No, but his gang will. I don't want to risk it right now—let's give it a while longer." Billy's stomach churned. "Mum reckons Eddy'll get sent to a youth detention centre for bullying us and stealing my birthday money."

"So, where to, then?" Ant shoved his hands deep into his jacket pockets. "Before we go anywhere, I need to go home for some gloves." Ant made a loud "Brrr," and shivered all over.

Billy scoffed, "What do you need gloves for? It's like midsummer out there, you big baby!"

"It's November, actually, and my mum says I've got bad circulation in my hands and feet. They get really cold." Ant held up his hands. "See, they're all blotchy red and blue already."

"Oh, diddums, you got freezing fingees and tootsies?" Billy sneered. "Let me have a look." He walked toward his friend.

"No, you're not being nice. It's not my fault, and anyway, they hurt when they get cold." With a step back, Ant folded his arms and buried his hands beneath his armpits.

"You're such a baby." Billy mocked. "How are you going to cycle like that? You won't even be able to reach the handlebars. I'll have to go without you if your fingees are too cold."

"Why are you being so nasty?" Ant sounded confused. He looked at his hand again, just to make sure.

"I'm not; you just need to grow up. All that 'my mum says' stuff is really babyish."

"Yeah, well, you can go for a bike ride by yourself, Billy Field." Ant's anger crackled in his chest. "You can be so mean." Ant turned and headed for the back door, but Jacko got there before him. "Sorry, Jacks, I've got to go." Gently, he moved the dog aside. "Not sure when I'll see you again."

Ant stroked the dog one more time. The click of the latch confirmed that he had left.

"Good riddance to bad rubbish!" Billy shouted after him. He knelt beside Jacko. "Who needs him, anyway? Come on, boy. Let's go walkies."

"I hadn't expected to see you back so soon." Ant's mum stood hanging out the washing when Ant rode into the garden. "Where's Billy? I thought you two would be out on your bikes."

Ant rode past his mum, stopping at the garden shed, and said nothing.

"Ant … Anthony, come here, now!"

Ant meandered across the garden; his hands plunged into his pockets. "What?"

"Don't what me. I was talking to you. What do you have to say for yourself?" His mum's face had lost its usual smile.

"Nothing." He dropped his head and kicked a stone between his feet.

"I asked you a question, and I expect an answer." She brought her eyes level with his.

"Hi, Mum. Hi, Ant." Maxine, Ant's younger sister, said as she skipped up the garden. "What are you doing, Ant? I thought you were going to Billy's." She skipped on by.

"Not now, Max dear," called her mum, but Max had already gone out of earshot. Ant started to wander off, too.

"Not so fast, young man. You've not answered my question." His mum folded her arms across her chest.

"It's nothing, Mum, really."

She stood her ground. "Well, if it's nothing, you won't mind telling me."

"Billy," Ant mumbled into his socks.

"What about Billy?"

"He called me a baby and said I needed to grow up." Ant shifted his weight from foot to foot.

"That's not like him. You two are best friends."

"We were." Ant's eyes sprang an unexpected leak.

"What have you done to upset him?" His mum looked stern.

"Why is it always my fault? Even when Max does something wrong, I get the blame. It's not fair." Ant let out a loud sigh.

"Look, no one's blaming you for anything. I'm just trying to find out what happened between you and Billy."

"It's because I said I needed gloves."

"Gloves?" She looked quizzical. "What's wrong with needing gloves?"

"My hands get cold."

"Of course they do; you've got poor circulation."

"That's what I told him." Ant shoved his hands deeper into his pockets.

"And that's why you two fell out?" His mum shook her head.

"He's ten now and thinks I should be more grown up like him. I can't help when my birthday is." Tears rolled down Ant's cheek.

"Here." She put her arms around him. "You're my big boy. Now, no more of this. Anyway, you've got Max to play with."

"Yeah, but she's a girl." While he spoke, he spun on one foot and wandered off toward the front gate, dragging his toes along the stone garden path. He walked past Max, who had just finished visiting their rabbit, Cinders.

"What's wrong with him, Mum?" Max smiled up at her.

"Oh, he just wants to be grown up," their mum said.

2

ANT FINDS A NEW FRIEND

A few days later, Max answered the ringing telephone. "Mum," she said, holding the receiver away from her mouth. "It's Katie's mum." She passed over the handset.

Her mum placed her hand over the mouthpiece and looked at Max. "Why's she calling?"

"I asked Katie here to play. Her mum wants to know if it's okay."

Max's mum sighed and took her hand off the receiver.

"Hi, Katie's mum—oh, sorry, I mean Jacquie. Yeah, that's fine. When's she coming?" She paused. "*Today*? And staying for tea?" She glared at Max.

Max nodded in agreement. "Please, say it's okay," she mouthed.

Her mum turned back to the phone. "Fine, yes. See you in a few minutes. Bye, Jacquie." She shifted her attention to Max. "Next time, young lady, how about a bit more warning? You're lucky I've made spaghetti. You can set an extra place at the table." She handed Max a knife, fork, and spoon. "Does Katie like spaghetti?"

Max shrugged. "Not sure. I know she doesn't like cooked carrots. At school, she always leaves them on the side of her plate."

Though nice to know, Max's mum wondered why her daughter had shared this information. The thud of a car door interrupted her thoughts.

Max and Ant raced to the front-room window. They both stood on tiptoe for a better view.

"Look, Tom's in the car." Ant said. He waved at Katie's brother. "Muuuum!" Ant hollered.

"Not so loud!" Max clasped her hands over her ears.

Their mum raced into the front room. "What's the panic?"

"Look, Tom's in the car," Ant said, pointing to his classmate. "Seeing as Max is having Katie over, can Tom stay, too? Please?"

His mum looked out of the window. "What? For tea as well?"

Ant pleaded, "Please, Mum. It's only fair."

She rolled her eyes. "Go on, then. Quick, get out there and see if he wants to stay."

Before she had finished speaking, Tom and Ant raced through the front door with Katie. Jacquie waved from the car and mouthed *thank you* at Max's mum.

After she'd closed the front door, all she saw were the children's backs disappearing upstairs.

"Keep the noise down! Tea's in half an hour." Their mum had no idea if they heard her.

All four children crashed into Ant's bedroom.

"You got an Xbox?" Tom asked and looked around.

"I've a PlayStation, but it's down in the front room." Ant bent to look under his bed. "I've got a Nintendo DS."

"We can't all play on that," Max said, helpfully.

"We could take turns," Ant said.

"Ant, we have guests. Mummy says we have to play nicely, all together."

"What about music?" Katie said, and then hummed.

Ant looked at the shelves above his bed. "I've got an old radio CD player thing.

Mum went to throw it away, but I asked her if I could keep it instead."

"Does it work?" Tom spoke as he examined it.

"No idea. I just thought it looked cool; it needs batteries."

"Have you got any CDs?"

Ant scanned along his bookshelf. "Nope, but I think Mum and Dad do."

"Oh well." Katie sighed. "It doesn't matter."

"I know." Max clapped her hands in excitement. "What about Simon Says?"

Tom had his hand up first. "Bagsie being Simon."

Max protested, "It's my idea."

"Yeah, but I said bagsie first." Tom looked at the others for support.

"Go on, then." Max pushed him forward. "We need to make a line." She gestured to Katie and Ant.

"Simon says stick your tongue out." Tom spoke; all three followed.

Ant brought his hands level with his ears and waved them for added effect.

"You're out, Ant," Tom declared. "Simon said only stick your tongue out."

Ant pouted and stepped out of the line. The game continued.

"Simon says stand on one leg."

Katie swayed before losing her balance.

"You're out too, Katie," Tom told her, and Ant nodded.

"That's not fair. I stood on one leg," she said, in a grump. "I'm just not good at balancing."

"Okay, you're still in, I suppose." Tom looked to Ant and Max. They shrugged.

Tom gave another command, "Wave your hands above your head."

Katie waved her hands. "You're really out this time," the other three said together.

"Right, children." Ant's mum stood at the bedroom door. "Hands washed and down for tea."

"This is delumptious, Mrs. Turner." Tom loaded up another forkful of spaghetti. "Thanks for letting me stay." He gulped, and sauce ran down his chin.

"Ant has seemed rather lost since he and Billy had their falling out." Ant's mum stared at Ant.

"Yeah, what happened, Ant? I noticed you two don't talk at school anymore," Tom added between mouthfuls.

Max chirped up, "Billy called him a baby."

"That'll do, Max. Billy is, I mean was, Ant's friend. You don't know what happened. You weren't there."

"Yeah, Mum, but Ant told me." Max pushed away her plate and dropped her shoulders. "He *did*," she huffed under her breath.

"It's because he's ten now, and he thinks he's all grown up," Ant said in a snarly voice.

Tom creased his brow. "Ten and grown up?" His eyebrows formed a long hairy slug.

"Yeah—I'm only nine. My birthday's not until March." Ant held up his fingers to count. "One, two, three. ... It's nearly six months after his."

"Well, I'm ten," Tom said. "Actually, I'm older than him. I'll be your best friend."

Ant broke into a broad grin, which proved difficult as he was in the middle of slurping up a long strand of spaghetti. He sucked with such force that it flipped up, hit his cheek, and left a streak of brown sauce. Each of the children had a try at slurping up their spaghetti. Laughter soon dominated the table.

"That's enough now, kids."

"Come on, Tom." Ant swung off his chair. "Let's get out the PlayStation." He felt keen to play with his new best friend.

"Not so fast. You need to ask to be excused before leaving the table." Ant's mum looked at Tom's plate. "He's not finished yet."

Tom gave a mighty slurp, and the last two strands of spaghetti disappeared from his plate and whipped around his cheeks. With his face looking like a cat with whiskers, Tom jumped down from the chair.

"Come here a second, Tom." Ant's mum had a paper towel ready. She managed a double wipe before he ran off. "I don't know what your mum would think."

Tom left, hot on Ant's heels.

3

BILLY MISSES ANT

At dusk, Billy walked around his back garden. A stiff breeze rustled through the branches and Jacko chased the falling leaves.

"D'you know what, Jacks?"

The dog strolled over to him.

"I miss playing with Ant."

Jacko's tail wagged at the mention of Ant's name.

"It's no fun playing by yourself." He stroked the dog. The question of what Ant was doing right now buzzed around inside Billy's head.

Billy sat on the back doorstep with Jacko beside him. The dog leant in, and his weight pushed against Billy's legs.

"I know!" Billy jumped up, making Jacko stumble. "I've got lights on my birthday bike." He opened the shed door and picked up his high-visibility jacket and helmet. "I'll cycle over to Ant's and find out what he's up to."

He wheeled his bike to the garden gate. "Stay here, Jacks. I'll only be ten minutes." Billy pedalled off, leaving the dog to run the length of the garden fence, woofing while Billy disappeared from view.

Billy's grandad's house stood just two doors away from Ant's. When Billy passed, he noticed that the curtains in grandad's front room hung closed.

That's good, he thought. *I don't want Grandad to see me; otherwise, he'll wonder what I'm doing.*

Billy slowed to a crawl when Ant's house came into view. He looked up at his friend's darkened bedroom window. Downstairs, it looked like a different matter. With the front room curtains open and every light on, Ant and Tom became clearly visible. They looked to be having great fun.

Billy came to a stop. He gawped, making his mouth look like a stunned goldfish. The two boys remained completely focused on their game.

"What's Tom doing playing with Ant?" Billy's surprise made him blurt out the words.

As Billy watched, Max and Katie joined the two boys. Billy ducked down below the hedge so that they wouldn't catch him peeking.

Billy had seen enough. He pushed hard on the pedal, and the bike moved off. He realised what losing a friend felt like. Tears ran down his cheeks and splattered into his lap.

"Billy." His mum walked outside, headed toward the dustbin. His bike lay on the ground with the lights still on. Beside it lay his jacket and helmet.

"What's this lot?" She got no response. "Billy?"

She looked up and down the garden. As she did, Jacko came bounding over. "Where's that boy?"

Jacko didn't answer.

Back in the house, she wandered from room to room. "Billy?" she called up the stairs. No response. Jacko stood alongside her. "Go on; you're a retriever. Go find Billy."

Jacko looked up at her with his large brown eyes but didn't move.

"Where is he? Fetch!"

Jacko wandered down the hallway, and then stopped outside the door to the under stairs cupboard. The door hadn't snapped shut, and he tried to hook a paw into the crack.

"What are you doing, you silly dog? He's not in there. Go on; find him."

Jacko stayed put.

"Billy?" his mum called out again.

Jacko scratched at the door.

"I've got no time for this." Billy's mum turned to walk away.

Jacko persisted.

"You'd better not be joking me," she said, ruffling the dog's fur.

Billy's mum bent down, pulled open the door, and peered in. The coat hooks lining the walls were piled high. The cupboard had no light, which made it difficult to see into the deep recess.

"Billy?" she called. "Are you in here?" Billy's mum waited, but no reply came. "Oh, I don't know, Jacko. You're imagining things." She stood back to close the door.

In an instant, Jacko disappeared inside.

"Jacko, come on; this isn't a game." She lifted a torch from the shelf. The bright light reflected in the dog's eyes. Beyond Jacko, Billy's mum could just make out the back of Billy's head, turned away from the probing beam.

"Billy, what on Earth are you doing hiding in here?" Her voice expressed both surprise and concern. "What's happened?" she asked. "It can't be that bad."

"It is." His mumble came out just about audible, but his long sniff sounded loud and clear.

"Hey, come on; you can tell me." His mum moved inside the cupboard. It gave her barely room to turn. "Let's get you out of here, and then we can talk more easily."

She reached out, and her hand made contact with his shoulder. "I'm too big to get to you. Billy, please. I hate to see you upset." She rocked him gently.

"Jacko, come on. Move." The dog did as she told him, and she edged closer. "What's all this about?"

Billy offered his mum his hand. She pulled him into a crouching position and held him steady. In the dim light, his eyes glistened with tears.

"Come on." Billy's mum guided him toward the door.

"It's my fault. I behaved nastily to him." Billy sniffed. His head sunk into his shoulders.

"Then, you should apologise, say sorry, and I bet it'll work out okay."

They reached the kitchen table and took seats. Billy held his hand to his forehead to shield his eyes from the bright light.

"Why did you climb into the cupboard?"

"'Cos he's got a new friend. They were laughing loads; I saw them." He dropped his gaze to the table.

"Is that where you've been? Did you cycle to Ant's?"

"Him, Tom, Max, and Katie all played together. I wanted to say sorry, but I couldn't with that lot there." His bottom lip quivered.

"You'll find another time," his mum said cheerily. "What about at school, in break time?" She looked for a reaction.

Billy shrugged. "Maybe, but he was the one who stormed off. He should say sorry to me."

"Do you want Ant as your best friend?" His mum sounded firm.

"Yeah, but it seems like he doesn't want me as his. Especially now he's got a new friend. It didn't take him long to forget me." More tears filled Billy's eyes.

4

BILLY LEARNS TO SKATEBOARD

The next day, Billy made up his mind to find his own new best friend.

"Mum, I'm off," Billy shouted as he closed the back door.

He stood outside, wearing his bike helmet, and his mum looked at him through the kitchen window.

"Where are you going? And who with?" She called after him.

Billy didn't answer.

Billy's mum ran to the front door just in time. "Billy, stop. I need to know where you're going."

He pulled up on his bike. "Oh, nowhere, really. Now I've got no mate, I just thought I'd go into town and see who's around." He turned his pedal back, ready to make his getaway.

"Haven't you got homework to do?"

"Not on a Saturday, Mum. I'll finish it tomorrow. I'll get back for lunch, promise."

"Have you got your cycle lock?" His mum fussed some more.

He tapped the cable wound around the stem of his bike seat.

"Key?"

"Come on, Mum; it's a combination lock."

"What's the code?"

"Ten-ten—my birthday. It's not like I'll forget it."

"Right, okay, but come back here for midday."

"Okay." He pushed his leg forward, and the bike moved off.

The shopping centre acted as a magnet for teenagers on Saturdays. The boys gathered at the seats under the large mechanical show clock, or at the burger bar, or sports shop. The girls had a different set of priorities, usually involving clothes, makeup, or shoes. Various groups moved between these locations, checking each other out and picking up the latest gossip.

Billy had no real interest in girls. He found himself outside *Boards and Bikes*, drawn to a display of skateboards. There, he surveyed the numerous boards with their striking, colourful graphics, and the arrays of wheel sets in dozens of colour patterns and sizes, and all the trucks and bearing combinations anyone would need to build their own skateboard. For the less ambitious, the shop had plenty of pre-made boards also.

"Look at *them!*" an older boy, standing nearby, exclaimed. His eyes grew wide like flying saucers. He stood pointing out a set of wheels to a younger boy, who looked like he could have been his brother. "Who'd put wide pro-wheels on Haslam 139 trucks?"

Both boys laughed.

Billy had no idea what they were talking about, or why they found it so funny. He smiled and nodded, thinking it the cool thing to do.

"Are you a skater?' the taller boy asked Billy.

"No, not really, but I want to be. I had a go on my friend's board once."

"So, you haven't even got a board?" he said.

"Only one of those yellow kids' plastic ones, but my dog chewed the wheels off. I looked through the *Boards And Bikes* catalogue yesterday; I want a board with Spitfire wheels and Burner Bearings." Billy felt proud of himself.

"Wow, that's ambitious. A good choice, but you need a board first. I've got Spitfires on this." He showed Billy his board.

"Awesome." Billy spun one of the wheels. It turned freely, without a hint of resistance. "Decent."

The boy gloated, "Yeah, and that's without Burners. You can't imagine what they'll be like when I get those."

"Can I have a go?" Billy asked before he realised what he'd said.

The boy looked at his brother. "What do you reckon, Woody?"

"Not here. He'd break his neck on this floor. It's too hard and smooth for a beginner."

Billy winced at the comment but said nothing.

"Fancy coming over the skate park?" the older boy said.

"Yeah, sure. My bike's in the rack; I just need to grab it."

The three boys walked toward the exit. "I'm Billy, by the way."

"Hi, I'm Dan, and this is my brother Edward, but everyone calls him Woody. We go to Elliott's School. I haven't seen you there." He looked Billy up and down. "Mind you, we don't hang out with year sevens."

Billy stayed quiet. He didn't want them to know his mum worked as Deputy Head Teacher, or that he'd only reached year five and remained at primary school. He stood up straight, pulled himself taller, and felt pleased to be big for his age.

"Can I hold your board?" Billy reached out to take it from Dan. He wanted to bring the conversation back to skateboarding. "Looks like you've had some scrapes on this. Can you drop and pump?"

"Yeah, of course. That's basic." Dan looked smug.

"Nice! Can you teach me?" Billy's enthusiasm sounded in his voice.

"We'll try.' Dan elbowed Woody. "He's pretty keen." The brothers exchanged glances.

"Okay, don't try nothing fancy. Stand sideways and put your back foot toward the end of the board and your front one pointing in the direction you want to go." Dan took hold of Billy's arm to steady him.

They stood in the half-pipe at the skate park.

"Now, bend your knees and push up, but put more pressure on your front leg to go forward."

Both nervous and excited, Billy followed Dan's instructions. He screwed up all his courage and pumped and made the board edge forward.

Dan moved with him. "Now, pump some more."

Billy progressed across the half-pipe until he reached the incline on the far side. He could feel the board wanting to roll back down.

"You've got to go back the other way." Dan still held Billy's arm. "Now, twist yourself around so that your back leg becomes the front, and you can see where you're going. Pump both legs again, but put more pressure on the front foot."

The board picked up speed, and Dan let go.

Billy rolled back across the half-pipe. He wobbled but managed to stay upright.

"Hey, you're a natural," Dan shouted as he caught up with him. "Now, pump again to go back to the far side."

With a bit of extra momentum, Billy rolled further up the half-pipe curve before accelerating down.

"Relax. Try and keep a steady rhythm."

While chewing on the corner of his mouth, Billy concentrated as hard as he could. The skateboard rolled to and fro. He felt desperate to impress Dan and his brother.

Both boys watched Billy. Getting more confident, Billy pumped hard until he got too cocky and fell.

"You'll have loads of falls if you get a board," Woody said. The brothers chuckled, and Woody rubbed his backside to emphasise what it felt like to learn.

Billy held his bottom; which hurt a lot. Determined not to let them see, he blinked back the tears.

"You okay, Billy?" Woody asked.

"Yeah, fine." He bit his lip, doing all he could not to show his pain. Then he ran after the board and tried to jump onto it. His combined weight and motion pushed the board across the pipe, up the curve, over the platform edge, and onto the grass.

"Steady, that's my best one," Dan said. He sprinted off to retrieve it. "I think that's enough for your first lesson."

"Does that mean I can have a go again?" Billy stared at Dan with his eyes wide. He felt so excited on the inside; on the outside, he tried to remain cool. "How about next Saturday, around eleven?' Billy asked hopefully.

"Let's say twelve, and I'll bring my old board for you to smash up." Dan and Woody sniggered.

"Come on, bro, we need to go." The brothers turned and waved to Billy as they walked across the park.

When he looked beyond them, Billy noticed Eddy's mates standing next to the swings talking to some girls. Now that Billy stood alone, he decided not to take any chances. He rode out the park's side entrance, preferring the longer but safer way home.

The following Saturday, Billy arrived at the skate park early. He sat astride his bike, resting one foot on the half-pipe ramp and the other on his pedal. *I might need to make a quick getaway,* he reasoned. All he could do now was wait.

Not wanting to get caught by Eddy or his mates, he scanned the park constantly. In the distance, three boys approached. The church bell rang twelve times.

That must be them, Billy thought. When they got closer, Billy recognised Dan and Woody, but not the third boy. He felt relieved that his new friends had turned up. Being in the park alone felt a bit scary. But who was the other boy? Fear nibbled at Billy's insides.

He watched all three figures move toward the skateboard ramp. Though definitely Dan and Woody, the third boy also looked familiar. A sharp pang of fear hit Billy when he recognised him; the boy hung around with Eddy's gang.

Billy hooked his foot under the pedal, bringing it to the top of the chain wheel for maximum getaway power. He didn't want to take any chances.

Of course, Dan would be the same age as Eddy, he realised. A lump formed in his throat. *What if he's found out about Eddy bullying me and stealing my birthday money?* His mind raced — he didn't know whether to stay or go.

"Hey, Billy." Dan had spotted him.

Too late to leave now. "Hi, Dan. Hi, Woody." Billy's stomach knotted.

"This is Stu. He's in my year," Dan said, patting Stu on the back. "He's the best skateboarder around here. He taught Tom, you know, Eddy Jost's younger brother."

Billy turned pale and felt sick at the mention of Eddy's name. As he suspected, Stu was friends with Eddy.

"Yeah, Tom and I are in the same year." Billy tried to remain calm, but he couldn't hide the tremble in his voice. "I haven't seen much of him recently. He hangs around with Ant Turner now."

"I know," Stu said. "Eddy's got Turner to thank for the trouble he's in, or his sister, at least. She got him caught, and now Eddy has to go to court." Stu held Billy's gaze. "Eddy doesn't hit girls," Stu said in a slow, threatening way while he moved closer to Billy. "But Turner needs to watch out." Spittle sprayed from Stu's lips, and his eyebrows knitted together. Stu's jaw pushed forward.

Billy dropped his eyes and inhaled to speak, but stopped himself before he could ask Stu what Eddy planned to do to Ant.

"Yeah?" Stu's response sounded menacing.

"Nothing. Anyway, Ant Turner's not my mate anymore." Saying the words out loud gave them added meaning, but Billy still felt unsure if he meant them.

"Come on, Stu," Dan cut in. "This isn't the time to sort it out. Anyway, Billy's our friend, and he seems like a good skateboarder."

Dan handed Billy his old board. "This is the one I told you about. It needs new gripper tape, and the deck's scratched, but it's fine for a beginner."

Billy turned the board over and looked at the underside. He ran his fingers along the edge of the deck before he spun the wheels. They wobbled a bit. He smiled, as he didn't know what he should look for. "It's great. Much better than my plastic kids' one." He stared at the board, wide-eyed.

"Take it for a spin," Dan offered.

Billy remembered what he had learnt the previous week. *This is it,* he told himself. He could feel all eyes on him. He pushed off and pumped to get across the half-pipe. The board seemed slower than the one he'd tried last week, but still good enough.

"Yeah, I like it," he called to them. He pumped again and picked up speed. This time, Billy whooshed across the half-pipe.

"See, I told you he was a natural," Dan said to Stu.

"Keep your arms at shoulder height, and don't lock your knees," Stu shouted to Billy, sharing the benefit of his knowledge.

Billy felt delighted with himself until the board hit the rail of the half-pipe's platform. It came to an abrupt stop, and Billy lost control. He tumbled backward and thudded down the curve. When he stood, it hurt loads, and he felt winded.

"The ... board's ... good." He had hardly any breath to speak. "It's just me who needs more practice." He sounded like a croaking frog. Determined not to show how much it hurt, Billy grinned through the agony.

"I'm selling it," Dan said casually. "I need the money for new bearings for my best board. I want about thirty quid if you're interested."

Billy looked at the board with new eyes, but he couldn't afford it. "I'd love to," he said. "But I only get four pounds pocket money a week."

"What about that twenty quid from your birthday?" Stu asked helpfully.

Billy's stomach tumbled. *I knew he was one of Eddy's thugs.* "I still haven't got enough."

"Won't your mum lend you some?" Dan asked.

"Not sure."

"But it's not really the money Dan wants." Stu looked at the two boys in turn. "It's new bearings." Stu rubbed his hands together like a pantomime villain.

"What are you suggesting?" Dan asked, cocking his head to one side.

"I mean, if Billy managed to get hold of some bearings, you'd give him your old board, right?"

"Yeah, I suppose so," Dan said. "And I'd let him have my old bearings for this board."

Stu placed his hand on Billy's shoulder. "How does that sound Billy boy?"

"What do you mean?" A chill ran down Billy's spine. "Me, steal them? I'm not sure I can do that." Billy arched his eyebrows and swallowed hard. He felt sick at the idea.

Stu stood back to watch his reaction. "That's up to you, Billy."

"I don't need to know how you get the bearings," Dan said. "But I'm happy to trade." He turned and signalled to Woody.

"We need to get home now. See you next week, Billy."

The brothers wandered off across the park, leaving Billy and Stu alone. Billy felt awkward. He hopped from foot to foot.

Stu mumbled, "Think about it." And then he turned and headed off.

Left alone, Billy's mind raced, and his thoughts tumbled around inside his head. Sweat seeped from his scalp, and rivulets snaked through his hair. *Steal?* he thought. *There must be a better way.*

5

BILLY EARNS HIS POCKET MONEY

In the school playground, Ant ignored Billy. Instead, he wandered over to Tom.

"If you bring your PlayStation controller tonight, we can play Sports Champions." Ant smiled at his new best mate.

"Sure your mum won't mind? It's the third time this week."

"It was her idea. And Katie can come, too," Ant said.

The school bell sounded, and the children lined up to go back to class. Ant and Tom joined the line.

Stood just out of sight, Billy heard Ant and Tom's conversation. He remembered what it felt like being best mates with Ant. *Yeah, well, they're just kids,* he thought. *I've got Dan and Woody now.*

Though Billy felt less excluded, thinking about Dan reminded him of Stu and what he had suggested. Billy's shoulders tightened, and his hands trembled. He had an urge to go to the toilet. *If I get caught. ...* It didn't even bear thinking about. *But I want the skateboard, and I want to be their friend.* The thoughts galloped through Billy's mind until he arrived at a plan.

"Oh, thanks, Billy." His mum couldn't hide her surprise at seeing an empty dishwasher. She shut the dishwasher door and smiled, thinking about what a good lad she had in her son.

"I've fed Jacko and cleaned all the dog poo out of the garden," Billy said, as he streaked through the kitchen and out into the hallway.

"Billy?" his mum called after him.

"Just a minute, Mum." He soon reappeared with an arm full of old newspapers. "Can you open the back door, please?"

Automatically, Billy's mum obliged and watched him work. He seemed like a whirlwind.

"Billy?" she tried again.

"I'm going to the recycle bin," he called over his shoulder.

Billy's mum stood in the centre of the kitchen with her arms held out, waiting for him to reappear. He did.

"Sorry, Mum." He sidestepped left, but she mirrored his actions. Then he ducked under her outstretched arm and raced up the stairs, taking two steps at a time.

Determined to catch him, his mum stood behind the kitchen door listening for him to come back down. The noises coming from upstairs suggested he was moving between rooms. Eventually, she sensed he was on his way. She waited, poised ready to pounce.

As he crossed the threshold, his mum jumped out and grabbed his collar. "Got

you! Now, what the heck are you up to?"
She held him tight.

Caught by surprise, he fumbled his load,
sending three wastepaper bins and their
contents scattering across the floor.

"Muuum!"

"Stop there and tell me what's going on."
Billy's mum held his collar tight, but he
struggled free.

"Look at me." She placed her hands on
his shoulders. "This is all very strange.
Usually, I have to chase you to do your
chores." She looked him in the eye.

"I know. I, er," he stumbled over his
words. "I just thought I'd be more helpful
now that I'm ten." He gazed back at her.

"Hmmmm," she said, looking him up and down. "What have you broken?"

"Nothing, Mum. Honest."

"I'll find out if you have." She thought for a moment. "You're not in trouble at school, are you?" She bent down, bringing her face close to his.

Billy dropped his gaze to the floor. "No."

"You don't sound too sure, Billy. Come on and tell me."

"Well, you know my pocket money?"

"Yeesss?" She wondered what would come next.

"You know it's for doing my jobs?"

"And?"

"I've still got two pounds left from last week, and my next lot's due tomorrow." Billy lifted his head.

"What do you want to buy?"

"Well, I've done next week's jobs already. The bins and recycling are every two weeks." He watched his mum for a sign of recognition. "Can I have my next week's pocket money tomorrow as well? Please, Mum? The bestest mum in the whole world ever." He threw his arms around her, hugging her as tight as he could.

She unclasped his hands and stepped back. "What are you up to, Billy Field?"

"It's just that Dan's selling his old skateboard." Billy's face glowed with excitement, and his eyes widened to twice their normal size.

"Dan? Dan who?"

"You know, he's at your school. He's got a brother called Woody."

She thought for a minute. "Woody? Do you mean Edward Prescott? Yes, of course, I know them both. Nice boys. How do you know Dan? He's in year nine."

"From skateboarding. I met him a couple of Saturdays ago in town. He's been teaching me." Billy was careful not to mention Stu.

"Why? How?"

"I was looking through the sports shop window—you know *Boards and Bikes*—when him and Woody got to talking to me about skateboarding stuff. Then Dan suggested going over to the skate park. Anyway, he let me borrow his board, and it turns out I'm quite good."

"And he has a board to sell, you say?" His mum wanted to be sure she had understood.

"Yeah, for thirty pounds. I've got twenty from my birthday, two I saved from last week, four from this week, and if you give me next week's pocket money early, I'll have the right amount."

"Yes, I heard all that, but is the board any good?"

"I think so. I've given it a spin. It's a bit slower than his best board, but he's promised me his old bearings once I buy his board off him. He needs the money to buy new ones." Billy talked fast as if he had been running.

"Are you sure it's what you want?"

He nodded vigorously. "And I've got Stu teaching me." In the excitement of the moment, Billy blurted out Stu's name. He flinched when he realised what he had said. "He's brilliant Mum; Dan says so." He hoped that might soften her reaction.

A look of horror appeared on her face. "You mean Stuart Dunderdale?" Her voice sounded shrill. "You need to keep away from him. He knocks around with Eddy Jost, and you know what he's like."

"Will you let me have my pocket money? Please?" Billy tried one more time.

"I'll think about it."

His mum said the dreaded phrase.

That's a no, then, Billy thought.

Billy pulled the duvet up to his chin. Jacko lay on the bedroom floor, just close enough to get stroked. While Billy played with the dog's ears, Jacko tried to lick his hand.

"I don't know what to do, Jacks. It seems my cunning plan won't go to plan after all." He dragged his fingers through the dog's fur. "Mum didn't actually say no, but my mentioning Stu ... what a big mistake."

Jacko yawned and dropped his head onto his paws.

"I can't sleep." Billy pulled his arms under the covers. "If Mum gives me the extra money, I can give it to Dan, but Stu will think I'm a wimp; just a little kid." He wagged his finger in the direction of the dog. "But if I steal the bearings, I'll be a criminal, and anyway, I'm bound to get caught." He wanted to be friends with Stu … sort of. Gloom set in.

Billy reached out to turn off the bedside lamp. The room fell dark, apart from a thin strip of brightness seeping under the door. Billy's eyes felt heavy, and Jacko snorted and snuffled. Then they both fell quiet; although, Billy's mind kept whirring.

"I know!" Billy sat bolt upright, and Jacko responded by jumping up and placing his nose in Billy's lap. "If I buy the bearings but *pretend* I stole them, the older boys will think I'm cool, just like them." Now that he knew what he had to do, he felt better.

Billy lay down again. "I don't want to be like Stu, and certainly not Eddy, but Dan and Woody seem nice."

Both he and Jacko fell asleep.

6

NEW WHEEL BEARINGS

"Thanks again, Mum." Billy jumped on the spot and clapped his hands. The ten pound coins jangled in his pocket; the twenty-pound note didn't make a noise. Unable to hide his excitement, Billy fastened the strap on his bike helmet, and then sped out of their garden gate.

At the shopping centre, Billy stowed and locked his bike in the cycle rack. It was still early in the day, he didn't want anyone to see him buying the wheel bearings. Fortunately, *Boards and Bikes* proved empty, and he made his purchase without anyone watching.

All done, he sat under the shopping centre's big clock to wait for Dan and Woody. To add to his deception, he took the bearings out of their bag and threw it, along with the receipt, into the bin.

The Prescott brothers came and stood beside him.

"Hi, guys."

"Well?" Dan bounced from foot to foot. "Have you got them?" He held out his hand. "Come on; don't make me wait any longer." He snatched at the box in Billy's lap. Then, holding it to his chest, Dan cherished it like a prized possession. His face lit up, and his grin stretched from ear to ear.

"They're only wheel bearings," Woody said, watching his brother in astonishment.

Dan stroked the box before removing the plastic film wrapping. Then he slid the inner box from its cardboard sleeve and revealed a set of eight gleaming steel ball races with their distinctive red inlays.

"Wow, Billy, these are awesome." He took one out of the box and held it between his first finger and thumb; he spun it.

Then he placed it next to Woody's ear. "Listen to that."

"I can't hear anything."

"Exactly! It's so smooth." Dan held it up for Billy to hear. "Come on, then; let's get to work."

Woody opened his skateboard's toolkit and passed Dan the bearing extractor.

"Get your old ones out, and I'll fit them to Billy's board," Woody said. Both boys beavered away.

Billy watched attentively, wanting to learn everything. "So, how come you know how to do this?"

"YouTube," Woody answered without looking up. "And my dad. He's always fixing things."

Soon, they had reassembled the wheels on both boards and got them ready to go. Dan placed his board on the floor and gave it a shove; not too hard, but enough to see it roll away with greater ease than expected.

He chased after it. "Come on, slow coaches. I've got to try it on the ramp."

Ant and Tom slowed their bikes when they reached the park gates. A woman with a yappy dog strolled by.

"Look who's over there," Tom bellowed, pointing toward the skateboarding ramp.

Ant followed Tom's finger and saw Billy. "So?"

"Come on, Ant; Billy's okay. You can't avoid him forever."

"It's him, not me," Ant snapped, feeling sad. His shoulders drooped.

"Well, Stu's there. He's my brother's mate. And Dan and Woody. Do you know them?" Tom pushed hard on his pedal.

Ant recognised Stu as one of Eddy's gang. Though hesitant, he had no choice but to follow Tom, even though his inner voice told him to keep away.

"What will Stu say when he sees me?" Ant's stomach tightened when he remembered the bullying incident.

"You'll be all right. Just stick with me." Tom pushed harder, and his bike sped across the park.

"Really?" Ant arched an eyebrow, he wasn't so sure.

The closer they got, the more nervous Ant felt. "Stop here." He laid his bike on the grass, preferring to walk the rest of the way.

🐕 🐕

"Where did Billy get that board?" Ant spoke from behind his hand so that only Tom could hear.

"No idea, but he's doing well. Stu's a good teacher. He tried to teach me a while back, but I never managed a drop." Tom studied Billy's technique.

Ant kept his distance, not wanting Stu to recognise him.

"You're good, Billy," Tom called out. "Where did you get your board?"

Billy didn't answer.

Tom turned to Ant. "He's just focused on the drop. They're tricky. Get your feet wrong or lose concentration and it's a wipe-out; you're bruised for a week." Tom laughed.

Both boys watched Billy's progress as he raced across the half-pipe.

"Nice one, Billy." Ant got caught up in the moment and spoke without thinking.

Billy said nothing, but Stu heard and looked over. Dan remained too busy with his board to notice.

Billy practiced a drop trick with Stu. The change of bearings had made a dramatic impact on the board's performance; it felt smoother, quicker, and more responsive.

"What's with you and Turner?" Stu said to Billy. "I thought you two were mates." He looked past Billy, directly at Ant. Stu stared at Ant like he was an alien with two heads.

"We were, but he's just a kid." Billy wanted to avoid talking about Ant.

"If you want to get into Eddy's good books, you could get back at Turner for him." Stu watched Billy's face.

Billy pushed his weight forward; committed, he managed another successful drop. Stu jumped down from the platform into the half-pipe and high-fived him when he skated past.

Billy stopped. "What do you mean?"

"Eddy's twenty quid short and not happy with Turner or his sister—or you, actually. But you've proved your talent for thieving." Stu glanced at Dan. Dan didn't see, as he stayed lost in his world of Burner Bearings. "If you steal Turner's bike, I know a bloke who'll give you twenty quid, no questions asked." Stu said it like it was the sort of thing he did every day.

"How, though?" Billy felt doubtful. "Ant's always with Tom, both at home and school."

"Turner likes skateboarding. What about next Saturday. I'll see Tom at Eddy's house and suggest he bring his new best mate over here again. You'll have to keep out of sight." Stu pivoted on his heels, looking for a place for Billy to hide. "See the Crazy Golf hut over there." Stu pointed at the hut. "I'll offer to help Turner learn a trick. Once he's off his bike, you make it disappear like magic." Stu beamed. "Easy."

Easy for you maybe, but I'm not a thief. Billy chose not to share his thought with Stu.

7

BILLY STEALS A BIKE

"Stu came around the other night." Tom kicked a stone across the playground as he and Ant headed toward the main school entrance.

Ant shuddered at the mention of Stu.

"He's not that bad," Tom said. "He even asked me if you want to have a go at skateboarding. He said to bring you along this Saturday, and he'll teach you some tricks. What do you think?"

Tom checked his watch; break time had nearly finished. "Tell me later. I've got Miss

Tompkins for PSHE, and she's always grumpy." He sprinted off across the playground.

Ant wandered back toward his classroom. Billy stood near the entrance. He wanted to ask him what to do about Stu. When he drew closer, Billy looked away. *You're not the only one who's mates with year nines,* Ant thought as he shuffled past. He made up his mind to go.

Saturday dawned a clear, crisp day. The sun came out, and the wind dropped. Piles of leaves heaped by the roadside. Tom and Ant enjoyed riding through them.

Tom came first through the park gate. "Look, Stu's over there."

Ant nodded. He pushed hard on the pedals to keep up with Tom. Several boys had gathered at the ramp, but Ant couldn't see Billy. It pleased him to be able to practice without his ex-friend seeing, but he felt surprised that he hadn't come. After all, it was Saturday, and Billy had his own skateboard now.

A pile of abandoned bikes lay near the ramp; Tom and Ant added their bikes to it.

"Stu!" Tom waved as he called to him. "Ant's just coming, but take it easy; he hasn't got much experience." Tom slapped Ant on the back and pushed him forward.

Stu ambled over to where Ant stood. "So, you reckon you can be a boarder?"

Ant hesitated. His cheeks glowed red.

Tom smiled. "Go on. Stu's the best around here."

Ant spoke softly, "I haven't even got a board."

"That's not a problem. I've got a spare. Now, watch me." Stu scooted to one side of the half-pipe. "You need to get up the curve, change direction, and come down again."

Ant followed his every move.

From the corner of his eye, Stu noticed Billy sneaking across the field with Ant's bike. Soon, both Billy and the bike had disappeared behind the Crazy Golf hut.

"Okay, one more time," Stu said, wanting to maintain Ant's focus. "So, scoot, pump, and shift your weight, then pump again. See, it's easy." Stu stopped where Ant stood. "Right, it's your turn."

He looked past Ant. The back end of his bike vanished between the two bushes that marked the path to the park's side gate.

Stu smiled inwardly; getting the twenty pounds would keep him in Eddy's favour for sure.

Billy rode Ant's bike the long way home to avoid Ant's road, and Tom's house, too, in case Max played outside with Katie. He just wanted to get the bike off the road and out of sight. After all, he had stolen his former best friend's bike. His sweaty palms slipped on the handlebar grips. Billy kept turning around, checking to see who watched, believing everyone knew what he had done. The thought of getting caught gnawed at his insides.

At the top of his road, he pulled up next to the bus shelter. Between it and the hedge, he found a gap wide enough to hide a bike. He used Ant's lock to secure it. They had bought the locks together when they were still mates and set the combinations as their birthdates.

I don't want anyone thieving it after all I've gone through to get it, he thought. Happy that it remained secure and hidden, he continued to his house. *I'll wait 'til dark and then move it to our garden shed.*

"Hi, Mum," Billy said as he came in through the back door. He tried to sound like his usual self while he removed his helmet.

"No skateboarding today?" His mum didn't look up from the pile of books she sat marking. "That's funny, I've just marked Dan Prescott's essay. A creative writing piece I'd set in class called, 'Do Dreams Ever Come True?' He certainly thinks so. He wrote three pages on his new wheel bearings and how they'll help him become a champion boarder." She smiled, pleased that Billy had become friends with the right boys.

"Yeah, great." Doubts about what he had done had followed him all the way home and continued to trail him as he walked up the stairs. Billy didn't feel at all pleased. He lay on his bedroom floor with Jacko curled around him like a blanket.

Billy wanted to get rid of the bad feelings and thought a play-fight might help.

"Come on, boy." Billy gave Jacko a gentle cuff around each ear, barely making contact. The dog swung from side to side, trying to catch his arm. They often played pretend fights. "You're not quick enough." He tapped Jacko first on the left side, then on the right.

Play fighting usually proved fun, but not today. Billy felt distracted, and Jacko seemed to know. The dog didn't bother to fight back; instead, he huffed before slumping down for a good paw licking.

"It's not good what I've done," Billy confided in Jacko. "Ant will have realised by now that someone's stolen his bike. Can you imagine how I'd feel if it were me?"

Billy understood Ant's loss so completely that he felt an unexpected and uncontrollable cramp in his stomach. Billy rolled onto his back and used Jacko as a pillow.

"Ant must be so unhappy."

From his pocket, he took the scrap of paper that Stu had given him and read it.

"Stan the Man, Richmond Road Industrial Estate."

He looked at Jacko. "Any idea where that is? Stu said something about it being on the left over the railway bridge. Apparently, Stan does house clearances." The only interest Jacko showed was a sniff of the paper. "Stan does anything for money."

"That's really poo." ... "Glad it wasn't mine." ... "Who'd steal a kid's bike?" And various other exclamations echoed around Ant's Monday morning classroom. Everyone seemed to know what had happened, and his classmates looked sympathetic. By break time, the whole school knew. Even Ant's teacher, Miss Tompkins, brought it up.

Deliberately, Billy avoided Ant, Tom, and their other friends. He kept to himself in the playground, mooching about with his hands deep in his pockets. He felt terrible and had no clue about what to do. If he had lost a prized possession, he would want his friends to support him. He couldn't support Ant, as they had fallen out, but having your bike stolen went well beyond anything he could imagine.

Monday dragged for Billy. To avoid the others, he spent his break in the library. At lunchtime, he offered to tidy the sports hall equipment cupboard, and in the late afternoon, when his teacher asked for a volunteer to deliver a pile of consent forms back to the school office, he got his hand up first. If he took the forms back to the school secretary, it meant that he could get out early, ahead of Ant and Tom. He didn't hang around.

Billy dashed straight home. As soon as he got back, he checked on Ant's bike. It remained safe, clean, and dry under the tarpaulin. As it wasn't his, he needed to get rid of it as soon as he could. The bike had to go, and now. Billy couldn't go through another day at school knowing the truth about what he'd stolen, yet keeping quiet.

Billy checked his watch: three-thirty. His mum wouldn't get back for a while. As Deputy Head Teacher, she never got home until well after school had finished. And Billy's dad wouldn't be back from work before seven at the earliest. Normally, he would go around to his grandad's house, but not today.

After he'd changed into in a hoodie, an old jacket, and ripped jeans, Billy put on his helmet but decided to leave his high-visibility vest on the hook. He didn't want to draw attention to himself.

The day moved toward dusk, and Ant's bike had no lights. Billy set off. The industrial estate lay about one mile away, on the other side of the railway tracks. Getting there meant using the bridge at the end of Ant's road, and going too near to school for Billy's liking.

"What if I'm seen?" He grew scared; his legs felt like lead weights and sweat droplets formed on his brow. As he rode, his arms shook, making the handlebars and front wheel wobble. The effort of pedalling felt exhausting, and no matter how hard he pushed, it seemed as if he wasn't moving a centimetre. Everything appeared to be closing in on him. He was certain he was being watched from behind each curtain, and that all car drivers were staring at him disapprovingly, positive he was up to no good.

He needed to swallow, but his mouth had gone completely dry. *This is the scariest thing I've ever done.* At the thought his stomach cramped, and his legs shook. Now he believed that someone unseen was following him. Without reason, he looked behind, and then in front, and then behind again. He saw no one but it made little difference; his panic built. *What if a policeman is standing around the next corner or over the brow of the bridge?* Billy's mind raced.

In his confusion, he failed to notice the Zebra Crossing ahead and kept going as if he had the right of way. On the crossing a lady with her Pekinese dog ambled along; she knew different. More through luck than anything else, he missed both the woman and the dog.

Billy heard a shout, "Be more careful," but assumed the shout must have been for someone else. The lady swung at him with her walking stick, and struck him across the back. The thump shook him and the intense pain was agonising, but he couldn't stop.

The railway bridge came into view. Billy felt relieved; he had nearly made it. The steep rise in the bridge hid what lay on the other side.

It proved a tough cycle to the top as Ant's bike had only three gears, and Billy refused to get off and walk. He pushed at the pedals extra hard. A sharp ache shot through his thigh muscles, but the thought of getting rid of Ant's bike drove him onward.

He made it; freewheeling down the other side felt good. *But not too fast,* he told himself. *It's on the left just after the bridge.* He recalled Stu's words.

"There!" He'd spotted a warehouse surrounded by high fencing. "Yes." He let the word escape. In the wire mesh fence a gate led into the yard. Secured above the gate, a large dimly-lit sign in blood-red lettering announced, 'Stan the Man', and underneath the phrase: 'Turn your unwanted goods into cash. Anything considered.'

Behind the cracked and filthy glass of the windows, a light glowed from within the building. Billy pulled up and watched. He could make out all sorts of stuff stacked high in the yard, but dusk made it difficult to see properly. He had no idea what anything was, and nor did he care.

The road seemed quiet with no cars or pedestrians in sight. Billy placed his hand on the gate's latch bolt and waited. He was unsure about going inside. It felt too creepy. His legs wobbled uncontrollably. *Come on. Do it… now,* he urged himself. He slid the bolt back, and one half of the double gate swung free. Billy readied the bike's pedal for a quick getaway just in case.

At the sound of a car coming over the bridge, Billy spun around. Its headlights picked him out, but the car didn't stop or even slow its pace. Billy sighed with relief. He checked up and down the road one more time.

Before he ventured in an outside light flicked on and the door to the building opened. Billy got his first glimpse of 'Stan the Man'. He had every right to feel frightened.

Stan saw Billy and shouted in a voice like thunder. "Oi, are you coming in or what?"

As he spoke, Stan started to walk toward Billy. His long thinning grey, almost white, hair pulled tight into a ponytail, swung as he moved. As Stan drew nearer, his height and bulk became clear; he seemed a giant. He stood over twice the height of Billy, with huge arm muscles and an enormous belly. He wore dirty blue overalls covered in oil and muck, and most of his face was hidden under a massive beard that wobbled as he chewed on a pencil.

The bellow of Stan's shout scared Billy to the core. He pulled the bike's front wheel back from the gate.

"Well?" Stan's gruff voice roared again.

The word rattled around Billy's helmet. In his mind there was no question, thought, or hesitation about remaining—he turned and took off like a frightened rabbit making it to the top of the bridge before Stan reached the gate.

Billy's legs ached, his breathing strained, his heart pounded, and he felt lightheaded, but he knew he couldn't stop however much it hurt. He continued to cycle as fast as the wind, even though the stitch in his side was big enough to mend the hole in the knee of his old trousers.

BILLY DOES THE RIGHT THING

Arriving at the bottom of Ant's road, Billy decided that the time had come for him to do the right thing. He'd had enough of feeling frightened and telling lies. Resolved, he swung the bike up the road and headed directly for Ant's house.

If I return the bike without getting caught, no one will know that I did it, he thought. Billy stopped at the garden gate. It had grown dark now. The curtains in the front room hung drawn, although a few beams of light escaped through chinks around the sides. He waited, listening for anything that might indicate danger. Then he hung around for a few more seconds. All clear.

Billy had been through the gate to Ant's garden enough times to know that the gate always scraped against the stone path. Gently, he lifted the gate as he pushed it open, and managed to do so noiselessly. He picked up the bike by the saddle and handlebars and carried it down the path. The street light failed to reach around the back of the house. The upstairs bathroom light cast a small pool of brightness in the garden, but nothing at all near the shed. Happily, Billy knew the way.

When he reached the shed, he peered through the window. It looked pitch-black inside. Ant and Max kept their big toys in there, and as usual, the family had padlocked it for the night. The combination lock hung snapped shut, but Billy knew the number. Ant didn't trust his memory, and so he had used his birthdate, just as he had with his bike lock. Within seconds, Billy had the door open.

The sound of blood pumping in his head blocked out any other noise. Billy focused on getting the bike back, and himself away, before he got seen.

Max was on rabbit duty. It was her turn to feed and water Cinders, and to change her bedding. The hutch nestled against the far side of the shed, away from any lights. When she heard the shed door open, she assumed that Ant had come outside. *I'll surprise him,* she thought. And, with that in mind, she snuck around to the window with the torch off and held under her chin, pointing up at her face. Max knocked on the glass and turned on the torch at the same time as letting out a scream like a witches cackle.

"What the heck?!" Billy dropped to the floor, sending a stack of toys flying. Frozen by fear, his stomach flipped. He had a gut-wrenching need to be sick.

"Ant? Is that you?" Max danced the light-beam around, making herself look even scarier.

She doesn't know it's me. If I stay still long enough, maybe she'll go away. Billy held his breath.

"Come on, Ant. I know it's you." She grew frightened and wished she hadn't played the trick. "Stop messing, Ant, and come on out. I know you're in there."

Where Billy had fallen, the bike pedal had jammed into his ribs. The pain took his breath away, and he needed to move to be able to breathe.

Max came toward the open door and shone the torch directly into his face. She gasped.

"Billy? What are *you* doing here?" She swung the light-beam around the shed. "That's Ant's bike!"

"Max, please. It's not what you think." Billy stood. He had no choice; the pain from the pedal became unbearable.

"So, how come you've got Ant's bike? I'm going to tell my dad." She turned toward the house.

"No! Max, wait." His brain raced. *I went down the canal and saw it dumped in some bushes, so I brought it back.* The words rushed from his thoughts toward his lips. His vocal cords tensed. *Once the words are out, I can't take them back,* he realised.

Billy hesitated, knowing more lies would only make things worse. He missed his friend, their computer games, their cycle rides, their dreaming about skateboards, and even Ant's awful jokes. *Why did I behave so horribly to him? The older boys aren't all that great. Well, Dan and Woody are, but ...*

"What do you want?" Max asked, edging nearer the house.

Billy watched her as she took another step.

"I'm going," she said, turning away.

"Can you get Ant?" Billy swallowed his words. "I need to tell him something. Please."

Max, torch in hand, disappeared through the back door. Billy stood staring, numb. He felt frightened but knew he'd done the right thing.

"Quick, Ant," Max ran into the front room. "I've got a surprise for you." Then she looked around and realised she'd spoken to an empty room. "Where are you?"

She ran back into the hall. "Ant? Mum, have you seen Ant?"

"What's all the shouting about?" Her mum appeared from the bathroom.

"I'm looking for Ant. It's important." Max carried on moving.

"Bedroom," her mum suggested.

The door stood shut, but Max didn't bother knocking. She flung it open, "Quick, Ant!" Only the streetlight lit the room, and her eyes needed time to adjust. "Where are you?"

"Here." Ant spoke in a whisper.

Max pirouetted a complete circle to find out where *here* meant. In the half-light, she stood on Ant's foot accidently.

"Yeeouch!"

"Sorry, bro, but you need to come quick." She bent and pulled at a foot.

"Leave me alone."

"Come on! It's important." She tugged his foot again.

"Get off me." He pulled his feet out of sight.

"It's about your bike," she said, jumping up and down and clapping her hands.

"What? Don't tell me; you know where it is? Yeah, right. Well, I bet you don't."

"I do, actually." Max jumped and clapped her hands again.

"Stop being horrible."

"I'm not horrible." She bent again and peered under the bed. "You'd better hurry, or your surprise might disappear."

Limb by limb, Ant emerged from under the bed.

"Come on." Max ran down the stairs. "Follow me," she called over her shoulder.

Billy stood Ant's bike in full view of the back door before retreating into the shadows of the shed.

Max switched on the kitchen light, and the garden lit up. She threw open the back door.

"See!" She stood to one side so that Ant could get a better look.

Ant's eyes widened, and his eyebrows shot up to his fringe. "My bike!" He ran to it and swung his leg over the crossbar. Seated astride it, he checked out the brakes, gears, and pedals. "'It's all okay." He tried the breaks again to make sure. He wore an ear-to-ear grin as he smoothed his hands over the paintwork, caressing his bike as if it were their pet rabbit.

"It should be. It's been well looked after." The words crept out of Billy's mouth.

"What?" Ant twisted left and right, trying to see who had spoken. "Billy? Is that you?" He hopped off his bike, his eyebrows now forming an angry V-shape. Hesitant, he wandered toward the shed.

Billy tried to speak but couldn't. It seemed as if his throat had closed over.

"Well?" Ant grew impatient.

"Sorry, Ant. I stole your bike." Billy croaked the words, but saying them made him feel better. At least it wasn't a lie.

Ant cocked his head. "But why?"

"Stu. Well, Eddy Jost, really. He said I needed to because Eddy wanted to get back at you and Max, and me, for getting him into trouble." Billy shuffled his feet and dropped his gaze. "And, I'm so sorry for calling you names. I just want to be your friend again."

"What about all those older boys?" Ant sounded confused.

"We can be friends with them when we're at secondary school."

"But you're great at skateboarding," Ant told him.

"Stu's a good teacher, but he's in Eddy's gang." Billy didn't want to think about them. "Anyway, how to skateboard is all on YouTube. Woody Prescott told me." Billy paused, then said, "Tom seems nice. You two have been hanging out a lot."

"Did you watch us?"

"Of course. I've seen you at school and here."

"Here?" Ant still looked unsure.

"I came around to apologise soon after we fell out, but you and Tom were playing computer games in your front room, so I couldn't." Billy stretched out his arm and placed a hand on Ant's shoulder. "When I saw you having so much fun with Tom, it made me determined to find a new friend. I know now that I've been stupid. I've missed being best mates with you." He smiled. "Especially your jokes."

"Oh, you'll like this one, then," Ant said, sounding more comfortable. He turned toward Billy. "Where do you find black holes? You'll never guess."

Billy rubbed his chin, pretending to think hard. "I don't know. Where do you find black holes?"

"In black socks, of course." Ant laughed aloud.

"Ha-ha, very good. I see your jokes haven't gotten any better." Billy smiled inwardly. It felt just like old times. "Remember how we promised that whoever got a skateboard first they would let the other one have a go? I haven't forgotten."

Ant smiled up at Billy. He'd missed his friend too. "Thanks for bringing my bike back. Can we forget what happened and be mates again?"

THE END

WHAT CHILDREN CAN LEARN FROM 'BILLY AND ANT FALL OUT'

In this book, we discuss pride. There are two different kinds of pride. The first is selfless and based on a person's achievements and qualities. Being proud of how we look, being part of a team or one's country gives us a feeling that comes from deep within; it uplifts us and makes us feel confident.

The other type of pride comes from our ego, which is arrogant and selfish and gives us an inflated opinion of ourselves—a sense of superiority. In reality, it makes us feel insecure and jealous and has us need to prove ourselves and impress those around us. Our ego thinks we have far more importance than we actually do, and therefore, will not allow us to admit when we are wrong or that we have made a mistake. We justify our actions even when we know they are flawed.

In the story, Billy is nasty to his best friend Ant, and they have a row. Ant goes away, confused by his friend's behaviour. He feels hurt and let down, and so he decides to find a new friend. When Billy sees how easily Ant finds someone else to play with, he feels abandoned, becomes annoyed, and convinces himself that he did nothing wrong. There is no way he will apologise.

The type of pride that we see in the story allows us to pretend that we're feeling good, strong, and confident, when in fact, we feel bad and guilty. Many negative emotions creep in when we allow our egos to take over: in this case, guilt because a best friend gets upset; jealousy that he's found another friend to play with; envy that he seems happier playing with someone else. Once these emotions take over, the ego works even harder to prove that whatever is happening is not our fault.

Yet if we're honest with ourselves and believe everyone is equal, we can understand that we make mistakes sometimes. Mistakes offer a way for us to learn; to know not to do the same thing again. If we think we're too important to be seen making a mistake, that's the ego coming out to play!

It is Billy's ego that entices him to go and find his own new friends to show Ant that he doesn't need him. Even though it feels a bit uncomfortable, he decides he'll show Ant that he does not need his friendship.

When the older boys draw him in and talk him into stealing, it becomes more serious. Then, worse still, they ask him to steal Ant's bike in exchange for money. By this time, he cannot untangle himself without losing face, and his ego won't let that happen.

However, Billy knows what he has done is wrong, and that things have gone too far. He doesn't want his friend to stay upset about losing his bike and tries to get it back to him without getting seen. When he gets caught, he realises that the only right thing to do is to apologise and try to get his best friend back.

The *confident pride* in himself that he is a good person overrides the *arrogant pride* that nearly caused him to lose his best friend. It takes courage to admit when you're wrong, but knowing that you can be honest about how you feel is the best reward there is.

Disciplining yourself to do what you know is right and important, although difficult; it is the highroad to pride, self-esteem, and personal satisfaction. **Margaret Thatcher**

A man's pride can be his downfall, and he needs to learn when to turn to others for support and guidance. **Bear Grylls**

GET YOUR FREE ACTIVITY BOOK

To accompany the Billy Books there is a free activity book for each title. Each book includes word search, crossword, secret message, maze and cryptogram puzzles plus pictures to colour.

To get your **free** Activity Book go to **www.thebillybooks.co.uk** and click the button **Get Your Free Activity Book**. Then click the cover of the book matching this book

BOOK REVIEW

If you found this book helpful, leaving a review on Goodreads.com or other book related websites would be much appreciated by me and others who have yet to find it.

READ ON FOR A TASTER OF

BILLY IS NASTY TO ANT

BILLY GROWING UP SERIES: JEALOUSY

James Minter

Helen Rushworth - Illustrator

www.billygrowingup.com

1

END-OF-TERM PROJECT

"Right, class, let's have some quiet." Miss Tompkins, year five's form teacher, clapped her hands to get their attention.

Best mates Billy, Ant, and Tom shared the same table. As usual, Ant sat telling a joke. He spoke in a soft voice so that Miss wouldn't hear him.

"If it takes one man one week to walk a fortnight, how many apples in a bunch of grapes?" Ant sat back, flashing a big gummy smile. "Well?"

Billy and Tom exchanged glances, before screwing up their faces in a *what's he talking about?* sort of way.

"You don't know, do you?" Ant grinned from ear to ear. "It's obvious, two elephants, of course." He sniggered.

Confused, Billy let out a mocking laugh. "You're weird." He spoke at the same time Miss Tompkins happened to be looking.

"Billy Field, that means you!" Her eyes narrowed, and she raised her voice to make herself heard.

"Sorry, Miss Tompkins." Billy's face turned red. The colour travelled to the tip of his ears. He did *not* like getting picked out by her; he always liked to think that he was her favourite. The last thing he wanted to do was cause her to get upset.

Billy looked down at his books. "It's your fault, Ant," he spoke in a whisper. "For telling such a stupid joke. Now, you've made Miss shout at me." Billy eyeballed him.

Miss Tompkins continued to speak, "Today, we will start our end-of-term project." She spoke in a slow, loud voice. "You will work in groups of three."

She moved to the front of her desk and leant against a corner. "You can choose who you want to work with and sit with them."

The sound of chair legs scraping on the wooden floor followed. "Not yet! Wait until I tell you." She eyed the class. "Right, now, quickly and quietly, move into your groups."

The noise in the room exploded with the sound of twenty-seven class members all standing at once. Billy, Ant, and Tom remained seated. As mates, they always did things together.

"I wonder what we'll get to do." Tom looked about him and pointed. "Have you seen Khalid? He's got to work with Julie and Suzanna. Poor him."

Billy turned to look. "I hope he likes boy bands. That's all they ever talk about." He smirked at the thought of Khalid's challenge.

"Okay now," Miss Tompkins called out to bring calm back to the classroom. "So, who's working together?"

She walked in the spaces between the tables, taking note of the different groups.

"Please, listen carefully. This project will count toward your individual assessment, but I'm also looking to see which team works best together, and which individual student contributes most to their team's efforts."

"She still hasn't told us what we're doing." Billy spoke out of the corner of his mouth so that Miss would not hear, but she did.

"Billy, not again! Now is not the time for talking." Miss Tompkins held his gaze.

"Sorry, Miss." He looked away, swallowed up by his embarrassment.

"I need one team member from each group to come to the front." Miss waved her hand in a *come here* gesture. "So, choose who you want to send."

A flurry of activity followed, as a race of children headed to her desk. Before Billy and Tom had time to discuss it, Ant had gone. He reached her first.

"Who said it should be him?' Billy asked, wide-eyed and glaring at Tom.

Tom shrugged. "I dunno; not me."

Ant returned, waving several sheets of paper. He set them down on the table, and all three boys leant in.

"This is awesome." Tom continued to read, and his eyes looked like flying saucers. "Create a TV-style advert. And look, it's a class competition where we get to vote on everyone else's." He jumped up and down in his seat.

"Yeah, but that means they'll get to vote on ours as well." Billy pointed to the paper.

"Look, there's an award for the team that produces the most creative thirty-second advert. And for the individual who makes the biggest contribution." *That will be me,* Billy thought.

"Cor, does it say what we have to advertise?" Tom could hardly get his words out with the excitement.

Before anyone had time to answer, Ant jumped up. "I know, let's do Rice Krispies. I'll be Snap." He did a little dance and made snapping sounds. "You can be Crackle," he said, pointing at Tom. "He's got blond hair like yours. And Billy, you can be Pop."

Miss Tompkins turned around to see what the commotion was, but Ant saw her before she saw him and sat down quickly.

"Phew, that was close." Ant took a peek to see if she still looked their way. "So, what do you think?"

"Really? Me as Pop?" Billy arched his eyebrows. "Why do you say that?"

Ant had no time to answer, as the racket in the classroom climbed to a new level.

Miss Tompkins' voice boomed out, "I know you're excited, but do you have any questions?" She rubbed the side of her head as if she had a headache.

The teacher peered over the top of her glasses.

"Look." Billy nodded to Ant and Tom. "She always does that when there's too much noise."

Gradually, the other children noticed, and the room fell silent.

Ant sat with his hand thrust high in the air. "Miss, Miss, Miss." He felt so determined to get her attention that his bottom hovered above the seat as he thrust his hand high above his ahead.

"Yes, Anthony? What have you got to say?" The grumpiness in her voice had gone.

"Miss, are we allowed to do the Rice Krispies advert? Please, Miss."

"I haven't agreed anything with anyone yet." She smiled at him. "Think about it a bit longer. Work out who will do what, and what costumes and equipment you'll need, then decide."

"Yeah, but I want to be Snap.' Ant jumped up from his chair and danced about.

"That's as may be, Anthony, but you heard what I said." She rubbed her forehead. "Please!" The word came out louder than expected, and everyone stared at the teacher.

Ant retook his seat.

"Have you noticed how Ant's been behaving with Miss?" Billy looked at Tom, keeping his back toward Ant so that he wouldn't overhear.

"What do you mean?" Tom looked past Billy and to Ant, who sat busy reading the handout.

Billy slumped back in his chair. "You know, he keeps going up to her desk, asking her questions and stuff like that. Even though he's made loads of noise, she's been nice to him, but she told me off twice."

"Maybe she feels sorry for him after he had his bike stolen." Tom sounded quite matter of fact.

Billy shifted in his seat. He didn't want any reminders of his part in the bike stealing, or for Tom to recall it either. His face reddened again until his cheeks burned.

Billy struggled to speak, "Yeah, you're probably right." *But I thought I was her favourite,* Billy kept that bit to himself. "What about doing an advert for toys, or …" He paused and thought, as he wanted to change the subject. "I know, what about doing one for games controllers? I wanted a new one for my birthday."

"Now, class, you've had plenty of time to

come up with ideas. Can one member from each group come to my desk—"

The crashing sound of a tumbling chair caused her to stop talking. Ant stood hopping about. In his haste, he had caught his foot on a chair leg and sent it flying. "Yeeouch."

Miss Tompkins shook her head in disbelief. "As I was trying to say, Anthony, can one member from every group come up to my desk and tell me what advert they're planning."

By the time she had finished speaking, Ant stood next to her. "Me, Miss. We … want …" He puffed. "… to … do … the … Rice … Krispies … advert." He panted so much that he could hardly get his words out.

Miss Tompkins picked up her pen. "I'd

never have guessed." Beside Billy, Ant, and Tom's names, she wrote, 'Rice Krispies'.

Ant dashed back to his table, avoiding any furniture or wayward chair legs.

"See, I said she would let us." He sounded triumphant. Then, seated, he beamed the broadest smile imaginable.

Billy and Tom exchanged glances; they both looked confused. "So, not toys or game controllers, then?" Billy picked up his pencil and doodled. "How come you decided? Who made you the leader?"

Tom wanted to keep the peace. "Yeah, but he did have the idea first, and he's done all the running up and down to Miss."

"Come on." Ant wouldn't be put off. He got out a pen and blank sheet of paper and drew a shape like a stage. "So, what do we need?" He looked at his two mates in turn.

"A box of Rice Krispies," Tom said.

"And a bowl," Billy said, helpfully.

"And milk. I like lots of milk on mine." Ant wrote a list. "What about costumes? Snap, Crackle, and Pop each wear a different colour."

As Ant spoke, Billy shut his eyes, trying to remember what colours Snap, Crackle, and Pop wore. He couldn't. "I think we'd better watch some TV tonight to remind ourselves."

"Their costumes won't be easy to make."

Tom groaned.

All three nodded.

I HOPE YOU ENJOYED THIS FREE CHAPTER. CONTINUE TO READ 'BILLY IS NASTY TO ANT' TO FIND OUT WHAT HAPPENED NEXT...

FOR PARENTS, TEACHERS, AND GUARDIANS: ABOUT THE 'BILLY GROWING UP' SERIES

Billy and his friends are children entering young adulthood, trying to make sense of the world around them. Like all children, they are confronted by a complex, diverse, fast-changing, exciting world full of opportunities, contradictions, and dangers through which they must navigate on their way to becoming responsible adults.

What underlies their journey are the values they gain through their experiences. In early childhood, children acquire their values by watching the behaviour of their parents. From around eight years old onwards, children are driven by exploration, and seeking independence; they are more outward looking. It is at this age they begin to think for themselves, and are capable of putting their own meaning to feelings, and the events and experiences they live through. They are developing their own identity.

The Billy Books series supports an initiative championing Values-based Education, (VbE) founded by Dr Neil Hawkes*. The VbE objective is to influence a child's capacity to succeed in life by encouraging them to adopt positive values that will serve them during their early lives, and sustain them throughout their adulthood. Building on the VbE objective, each Billy book uses the power of traditional storytelling to contrast negative behaviours with positive outcomes to illustrate, guide, and shape a child's understanding of the importance of values.

This series of books help parents, guardians and teachers to deal with the issues that challenge children who are coming of age. Dealt with in a gentle way through storytelling, children begin to understand the challenges they face, and the importance of introducing positive values into their everyday lives. Setting the issues in a meaningful context helps a child to see things from a different perspective. These books act as icebreakers, allowing easier communication between parents, or other significant adults, and children when it comes to discussing difficult subjects. They are suitable for KS2, PSHE classes.

There are eight books are in the series. Suggestions for other topics to be dealt with in this way are always welcome. To this end, contact the author by email: james@jamesminter.com.

*Values-Based Education, (VbE) is a programme that is being adopted in schools to inspire adults and pupils to embrace and live positive human values. In English schools, there is now a Government requirement to teach British values. More information can be found at: www.valuesbasededucation.com/

BILLY GETS BULLIED

Bullies appear confident and strong. That is why they are scary and intimidating. Billy loses his birthday present, a twenty-pound note, to the school bully. With the help of a grown-up, he manages to get it back and the bully gets what he deserves.

BILLY AND ANT FALL OUT

False pride can make you feel so important that you would rather do something wrong than admit you have made a mistake. In this story, Billy says something nasty to Ant and they row. Ant goes away and makes a new friend, leaving Billy feeling angry and abandoned. His pride will not let him apologise to his best friend until things get out of hand.

BILLY IS NASTY TO ANT

Jealousy only really hurts the person who feels it. It is useful to help children accept other people's successes without them feeling vulnerable. When Ant wins a school prize, Billy can't stop himself saying horrible things. Rather than being pleased for Ant, he is envious and wishes he had won instead.

BILLY AND ANT LIE

Lying is very common. It's wrong, but it's common. Lies are told for a number of different reasons, but one of the most frequent is to avoid trouble. While cycling to school, Billy and Ant mess around and lie about getting a flat tyre to cover up their lateness. The arrival of the police at school regarding a serious crime committed earlier that day means their lie puts them in a very difficult position.

BILLY HELPS MAX

Stealing is taking something without permission or payment. Children may steal for a dare, or because they want something and have no money, or as a way of getting attention. Stealing shows a lack of self-control. Max sees some go-faster stripes for her bike. She has to have them, but her birthday is ages away. She eventually gives in to temptation.

BILLY SAVES THE DAY

Children need belief in themselves and their abilities, but having an inflated ego can be detrimental. Lack of self-belief holds them back, but overpraising leads to unrealistic expectations. Billy fails to audition for the lead role in the school play, as he is convinced he is not good enough.

BILLY WANTS IT ALL

The value of money is one of the most important subjects for children to learn and carry with them into adulthood, yet it is one of the least-taught subjects. Billy and Ant want skateboards, but soon realise a reasonable one will cost a significant amount of money. How will they get the amount they need?

BILLY KNOWS A SECRET

You keep secrets for a reason. It is usually to protect yourself or someone else. This story explores the issues of secret-keeping by Billy and Ant, and the consequences that arise. For children, the importance of finding a responsible adult with whom they can confide and share their concerns is a significant life lesson.

MULTIPLE FORMATS

Each of the Billy books is available as a **paperback**, as a **hardback** including coloured pictures, as **eBooks** and in **audio**-book format.

COLOURING BOOK

The Billy Colouring book is perfect for any budding artist to express themselves with fun and inspiring designs. Based on the Billy Series, it is filled with fan-favourite characters and has something for every Billy, Ant, Max and Jacko fan.

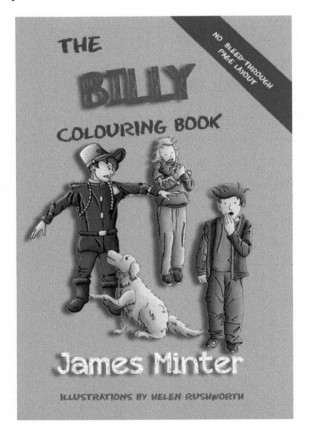

THE BILLY BOOK'S COLLECTIONS
VOLUMES 1 AND 2

For those readers who cannot wait for the next book in the series, books 1, 2, 3, and 4 are combined into a single work —The Billy Collection, Volume 1, whilst books 5, 6, 7, and 8 make up Volume 2.

The collections are still eligible for the free activity books. Find them all at www.thebillybooks.co.uk.

ABOUT THE AUTHOR

I am a dad of two grown children and a stepfather to three more. I started writing five years ago with books designed to appeal to the inner child in adults - very English humour. My daughter Louise, reminded me of the bedtime stories I told her and suggested I write them down for others to enjoy. I haven't yet, but instead, I wrote this eight-book series for 7 to 9-year-old boys and girls. They are traditional stories dealing with negative behaviours with positive outcomes.

Although the main characters, Billy and his friends, are made up, Billy's dog, Jacko, is based on our much-loved family pet, which, with our second dog Malibu, caused havoc and mayhem to the delight of my children and consternation of me.

Prior to writing, I was a college lecturer and later worked in the computer industry, at a time before smartphones and tablets, when computers were powered by steam and stood as high as a bus.

WEBSITES

www.billygrowingup.com

www.thebillybooks.co.uk

www.jamesminter.com

E-MAIL

james@jamesminter.com

TWITTER

@james_minter

@thebillybooks

FACEBOOK

facebook.com/thebillybooks/

facebook.com/author.james.minter

ACKNOWLEDGEMENTS

Like all projects of this type, there are always a number of indispensable people who help bring it to completion. They include Christina Lepre, for her editing and incisive comments, suggestions and corrections. Harmony Kent for her proofreading, and Helen Rushworth of Ibex Illustrations, for her images that so capture the mood of the story. Gwen Gades for her cover design. And Maggie, my wife, for putting up with my endless pestering to read, comment and discuss my story, and, through her work as a personal development coach, her editorial input into the learnings designed to help children become responsible adults.

Lightning Source UK Ltd.
Milton Keynes UK
UKHW011118250319
339732UK00001B/1/P